As a little boy I loved hearing the nonsense verse of Edward Lear, especially "The Owl and the Pussy-cat." Illustrated by Lear himself, the poem was intriguing but had few drawings. . . . I wanted to see more. More of the voyage of the pea-green boat and more of the inhabitants of the land of Bong. But it would be years before I found an opportunity.

After the Eloise books were firmly launched, I began a series of portraits of friends and celebrities, imagining them as birds, beasts, and even insects. One of my subjects was the well-known pussy-cat Bernadette Peters. When she came to my studio and posed with my Skeezix, I "metamorphosed" her into a cat, and found my path into Edward Lear's poem.

—Hilary Knight, July 2000

Skeezix & Bernadette

What an honor to be part of the retelling of this charming story. It has always been one of my favorites, and to be "morphed" by Hilary Knight was a special treat.

—Bernadette Peters

The OWL and The PUSSY-CAT

WELCOME TO
Professor
COMFORT'S
Story & Music
Hour

ASSISTED BY
ARABELLA

for
Michael
Patrick
Hearn

Hilary Knight's

The Owl and The Pussy-Cat

BASED ON THE POEM BY EDWARD LEAR

SIMON & SCHUSTER BOOKS FOR YOUNG READERS
NEW YORK   LONDON   TORONTO   SYDNEY   SINGAPORE

EDWARD
LEAR
1812-1888

SIMON & SCHUSTER BOOKS FOR YOUNG READERS
An imprint of Simon & Schuster Children's Publishing Division
1230 Avenue of the Americas, New York, New York 10020

Book design by Jennifer Reyes
The text of this book is set in Garamond.
Printed in the United States of America
10 9 8 7 6 5 4 3 2 1
The Library of Congress has cataloged
a previous edition as follows:
Knight, Hilary.
Hilary Knight's The owl and the pussy-cat.
Summary: Captivated by Edward Lear's poem, a boy
and girl turn into the owl and the pussy-cat and set sail
in a pea green boat for the land where the Bong-tree grows.
1. Children's poetry, English. [1. Nonsense verses. 2. English
poetry] I. Lear, Edward, 1812–1888. Owl and the pussy-cat. II.
Title: Owl and the pussy-cat.
PR4879.L209   198W3b   821'.914   83-9844
ISBN 0-689-83927-8

"Arabella! Warm up the muffins and cocoa. . . .

Our guests have arrived!"

"Is everything shipshape?...

I have the perfect story for you!"

"Otto and Polly, let's go on a voyage . . .

with the Owl and the Pussy-cat."

The Owl and the Pussy-cat went to sea
    In a beautiful pea-green boat.
They took some honey, and plenty of money,
    Wrapped up in a five-pound note.
The Owl looked up to the stars above,
    And sang to a small guitar,
"O lovely Pussy! O Pussy, my love,
    What a beautiful Pussy you are,
        You are,
        You are!
    What a beautiful Pussy you are!"

Pussy said to the Owl, "You elegant fowl!
    How charmingly sweet you sing!
O let us be married! too long we have tarried:
    But what shall we do for a ring?"
They sailed away, for a year and a day,
    To the land where the Bong-tree grows
And there in a wood a Piggy-wig stood
    With a ring at the end of his nose,
            His nose,
            His nose,
With a ring at the end of his nose.

"Dear Pig, are you willing to sell for one shilling
　　　Your ring?" Said the Piggy, "I will."
So they took it away, and were married next day
　　　By the Turkey who lives on the hill.
They dined on mince, and slices of quince,
　　　Which they ate with a runcible spoon;
And hand in hand, on the edge of the sand,
　　　They danced by the light of the moon,
　　　　　　The moon,
　　　　　　The moon,

They danced by the light of the moon.

"All together now!"

The Owl and the Pussy-cat went to sea.
in a beautiful pea-green boat.
They took some honey, and plenty of money
wrapped up in a five-pound note.

Pussy said to the Owl,

'You elegant fowl!
How charmingly
sweet you sing!
O let us be married!
too long we
have tarried:
But what shall we
do for a ring?'

JANUARY 1st

And there in a wood a Piggy-wig stood with a ring at the end of his nose,

His nose, His nose, with a ring at the end of his nose.

"Dear Pig, are you willing to sell for one shilling your ring?"

PIGS WOOD

Madame Chatte
FOR VEILS · GOWNS

Said
the Piggy,
"I will."

So they took it away, and were
married next day by the Turkey

who lives on the hill.

They dined on mince,
and slices of quince,
which they ate with
a runcible spoon;

And
hand in hand,
on the edge of
the sand,
They danced by the
light of the moon,
The moon,
The moon,

Otto,
Otto!
Dinner's
ready.

They danced
by the light
of the
moon.

PROFESSOR
COMFORT
says
GOOD
NIGHT